Amazing Angie..
City Ween

Rita Weyls

AuthorHouse™
1663 Liberty Drive
Bloomington, IN 47403
www.authorhouse.com
Phone: 1 (800) 839-8640

Published by AuthorHouse 07/19/2019

ISBN: 978-1-7283-2016-8 (sc)
ISBN: 978-1-7283-2017-5 (e)

Library of Congress Control Number: 2019910159

Print information available on the last page.

Any people depicted in stock imagery provided by Getty Images are models,
and such images are being used for illustrative purposes only.
Certain stock imagery © Getty Images.

This book is printed on acid-free paper.

Because of the dynamic nature of the Internet, any web addresses or links contained in this book may have changed
since publication and may no longer be valid. The views expressed in this work are solely those of the author and do
not necessarily reflect the views of the publisher, and the publisher hereby disclaims any responsibility for them.

authorHOUSE®

Dedication

This book is for Michael, Kent, Abby, Jack, Hudson, Bates, Violet and Dylan Frances.

Love,
Grandma

Chapter 1:

My name is Angie and I'm standard size, black and tan, silver-dappled, 5 year-old Dachshund. I have one blue eye and one brown eye. I live In the city of Brooklyn, NY., but that's all about to change very soon. Mom is packing up my stuff to get me ready for the long trip far away to my new home. My mom and dad have to move and the new apartment that suits them best, does not allow dogs. I guess they do allow gold fish and birds. Like what's that about?

Chapter 2:

I'm a very independent girl and I know my way around town unbelievably well. I know my way to the corner market and the neighborhood veterinarian and the cool park where all the children play. I could do this with no help at all, but I must let my mom and dad think they need to put me on the leash. That's ok, because it makes them feel safe and responsible. One day, I walked to the corner alone and the nice lady in the bakery shop gave me a big cookie. It's the best smell in the world. Mom never knew. She thought I was in the backyard. Much better that way. Everyone on the block stops to pet me, because, after all, I am Amazing Angie.

Chapter 3:

My dad's parents, or my new grandma and grandpa, will be taking me to the suburbs of Lakewood, Ohio. I wonder, just what is Ohio and is it even on the same planet as the exciting New York. I will soon find out as the grandparents are coming to pick me up. My mom and dad say that I will have two playmates there. My dad says they are rescue dogs and love being with grandma and grandpa. I can only imagine. I've heard mom and dad say they are two smelly, old boy dogs, too. Well, not the smelly part. The idea of it makes me laugh. I will have to teach them some new tricks. I wonder how I'm gonna' fit in.

Chapter 4:

Uh oh...they have arrived. Ok, they look nice enough, but this is going to be hard for everyone of us. We say our good-byes and my mom cries a lot. She has packed up my bed, blankets and winter coats. I know she is very sad. My dad tries to console her as he hands grandma a bag of my food and treats. Being Amazing Angie, I give mom's face a good lick and dutifully allow myself to be lifted into the back seat of the big car. I wear my most serious face. They have nice blankets and a bone for me. I'm a brave girl, but do have to wonder what's in store for me in the suburbs. I have to admit, I'm a little scared.

Chapter 5:

We stop many times along the way to my new home. They walk me on some grass at the rest stops so I can go pee-pee. They give me water and treats. Grandma and grandpa have soda and sandwiches. This is my first time on these big roads with huge trucks whizzing by. My grandma holds me and tells me everything will be fine. She assures me that I will be loved and spoiled just as much as the two smelly boys. Do I believe her? No, I do not. I'm a lot smarter than they think. Just wait till I show them what I can do.

Chapter 6:

At last, we arrive in Lakewood, Ohio. Oh no, I see them peeking out the front window now. One looks like a Holstein cow. He has black and white spots and long skinny legs and a fat tummy. The other one is little and tan and feisty. I think he's one of those, you know, what they call a lap dog. Yes, he's a Chihuahua and he won't stop barking at me. I could squish the little one with one of my strong paws, but I have good manners. His name is Pedro Oliver. Pedro Oliver?? What a ridiculous name. The 'cow' is named Sparky D and he's afraid of me. Hahahahaha. He's a rat terrier. I know this because there was one in my old neighborhood. I will have to take over in this house. These boys are clueless.

Chapter 7:

I'm missing my mom and dad a lot, but I won't refuse my dinner. Oh my! Pedro Oliver is trying to eat my food. I growl at him and he backs off. After all, I have dealt with much tougher, bigger dogs in my old hood. Sparky D is quite timid and let's me eat his food as well as my own. Can't have that. My grandma catches me and sends me back to my own bowl. Not a good sign. The old lady is too sharp. Stockpiling food is one of my best tricks. How will they know I'm Amazing Angie if I can't even sneak some extra food?

Chapter 8:

It's bedtime for our little family. We had a nice evening where I was placed on the couch by grandma while she and grandpa watched some really silly shows that I have never seen before. Now, I'm used to sleeping in my mom and dad's bed, but I get the feeling it's not going to happen here. My grandma takes my old bed and places it next to her big bed. I have to sleep alone for the first time in since forever! I guess they don't know yet that I'm Amazing Angie and I could protect them if only I could sleep with them. Oh I try, but my legs are too short for me to make the leap. So, I do the next best thing. I stand next to grandma's side of the bed and I stare her down. Grandma won't budge. She gently lifts me back into my bed. Ok, I'm tired and go to sleep. I do have good manners, but you already know that.

Chapter 9:

Yippee! It's morning and I had a pretty peaceful night. Thank heaven grandma didn't put me in the room with the two smelly boy dogs. We go for a morning walk and I get to scope out the new neighborhood. I'm strutting my stuff and already leading the way. I see a black Lab on the other side of the street and decide to ignore him. He's another clueless, smelly boy dog. The smelly boys follow me, cautiously. We walk all the way down the block and I already know my way home. Breakfast awaits. No, I won't try to take Sparky D's food again. I have learned my lesson. Can't be too pushy. Remember, I have good manners.

Chapter 10:

A week has passed and I like to play in the big backyard with the woods behind it. The smelly boys like chasing me around. I patiently show them how to open the screen door and pantry door with my nice, long nose. Sometimes, I hide my ball in there where grandma can't see it. The smelly boys can't figure out how I do this. I also show them where the snacks are kept. I can sneak into the pantry and take them from the bag. I have already hidden some snacks in the smelly boys' beds. We can have them when grandpa and grandma are out working in the garden. Yes, that's what I call them. I think their names are silly. Smelly boys works a lot better for me. Grandpa throws me my ball and I fetch. I love to play ball and have every color you can imagine. They say dogs don't see colors, but I can. I prefer the red and yellow ones to the blue and green ones. If this helps to make me amazing, then all the better.

Chapter 11:

I think I'm gonna like it here. Good food, good grandma and grandpa and ok smelly boys. So far, so good. I fall asleep in my bed, with dreams of more treats, more walks and lots of brightly colored balls to chase! Grandma and grandpa think I'm a genius when I catch the ball in the air. Like I told you before, I prefer the red and yellow ones. I even let Sparky D lick my face. He's a loving boy and this makes him happy. Pedro Oliver still tries to take my food. We have to work on that. Just yesterday, grandma and grandpa could not find Pedro Oliver. They were running all over the house calling that silly name, when I went over to the garage door and stood quietly waiting. I gave grandma the look. Then, I stared at the door and back at her. Then grandma, then the door. She got it, finally. Pedro Oliver had gotten himself locked in the garage and I was the one who found him. Guess he and I are friends now. Soon it will be bedtime again.

Chapter 12:

Oh no! I awaken to a strange smell. I look around the bedroom and grandma and grandpa are fast asleep. Grandpa snores and grandma sort of rolls him over on his side. It's a funny sight. Back to the smell. Nobody seems to be stirring. I'm Angie on the spot. I go to the sliding glass door which leads to my big backyard. That's when I see it. There's a huge fire in the woods behind us. I begin barking my head off. Soon grandma and grandpa are awake. Grandma says a few minutes more and the fire would have spread to the houses. It's coming quickly and is already in our yard. The firemen come with their big trucks and hoses and ladders. By now, most of the neighborhood has gathered around my house. I'm feeling quite proud if I do say so myself.

Chapter 13:

grandma and grandpa are standing outside with me and the two smelly boys. Several of the neighbors are asking how we knew there was a fire in our woods. My grandpa proudly tells everyone that I awakened them with my loud bark and my banging against the sliding glass door. I am the heroine of the hour or maybe even of the year. All the neighbors come over to pat me on my shiny, black head. The firemen stomp over in their big boots and say I would make a great firehouse dog. Even the old, black lab is there with his mom and dad. He gives me a sniff and big kiss. I politely wag my tail, but have no intention of moving from this great house. Moving was a little scary, but I was true to my new family and to myself. Yes, I love it here. I saved the day, because, like I said, I'm Amazing Angie.

CPSIA information can be obtained
at www.ICGtesting.com
Printed in the USA
BVHW021001290719
554569BV00008B/357/P